CW00863332

Website: scottytherescuedog.com
email: scottytherescuedog@gmail.com
Instagram: Scottytherescuedog

Scotty Runs for Mayor

The Adventures of Scotty the Rescue Dog

Written and Illustrated by Tammi Janiga

Relaxing in his hammock, enjoying the sea breeze, Scotty dozed off. He dreamt about what it would be like to be the Mayor of Dogedin.

To be the Mayor of Dogedin, Scotty must be a United States Citizen. He was born in the state of Florida.

He must be 25 years old. He is five in dog years. One dog year equals seven human years.
5 x 7 = 35.

He must live in the county he wants to be Mayor of for one year. He found his furever home precisely 2 years ago this month.

Scotty IS qualified to run for the Mayor of Dogedin!

MAYOR CHECKLIST
UNITED STATES CITIZEN
MUST BE 25 IN DOG YEARS
MUST LIVE IN DOGEDIN
5 human years
x 7 dog years
= 35

Scotty went to Dogedin City Hall to tell the clerk he would like to run for Mayor. He completed some paperwork to get his name on the ballot.

A Mayor needs a good Campaign Manager (someone to do all the planning), a Treasurer (someone to count the dog bones), and a Deputy Mayor (someone who can fill in for him).

Scotty asked his best friend, Pico, to be his Campaign Manager. He speaks Spanish as well as English. Pico is charming and well-liked, so he is ideal for the job. He accepted the invitation and is very excited to join the team.

Scotty asked Lacey to be his Treasurer. She is organized and very good at math. Lacey would be an ideal team member to count all the dog bones. She accepted his invitation to count and keep track of the dog treasures.

He asked Bear to be his Deputy Mayor. His job is to act as Mayor until a new Mayor is elected, if Scotty were unable to do his job. Bear is strictly business and would take this job very seriously. Bear happily accepts the offer to be Deputy Mayor.

Scotty picked up a blank notebook from the City Clerk. He needs to get 500 signatures from the citizens of Dogedin to run for Mayor. Once Scotty has collected enough signatures, he will give them to the City Clerk to accept his nomination.

Scotty has been working with Pico to design a campaign message. They have a new website, booklets, and buttons to spread the word to voters.

He needs a campaign slogan. He wants everyone to know he will help his fellow dogs in the Dogedin community.

"I've got it," Pico said.

"Scotty won't sleep until there is a bone in every bowl!"

YES!!! That's it!

"We will create a dog, friendly community."

"We need to raise money for your campaign, Scotty," said Pico.
They found some recycled plywood and built a dog kissing booth! "We will set it up in the dog park!" said Lacey. Bear painted the finishing touches on it.

Another fundraising idea is to set up a dog bubble bath in the park. For a small contribution, each dog will be washed, rinsed, brushed, and taken for a walk. He asked for volunteers in the community for their help.

Dog Wash Fundraiser

"We will pass out campaign buttons and flyers everywhere we go." said Pico "Vote for Scotty. Mayor of Dogedin"

Pico scheduled Scotty to make TV and radio appearances.

The team ran a good campaign, and they are exhausted. Everyone worked hard to help Scotty become the Mayor of Dogedin. All they can do now is wait for the voting results.

It's Election Day.

The ballots have been counted.

SCOTTY WON!

HE IS THE NEW MAYOR OF DOGEDIN!!!

HIP HIP HOORAY!!!

Thanks to all my canine friends for their support in my successful bid to become mayor of Dogedin. Special thanks to Pico, my campaign manager, and Lacey, my treasurer, for their hard work. As you all know, it has been a "ruff" campaign running for mayor. However, we overcame many obstacles to "unleash" our vision for a better Dogedin.

Thanks to my incredible team, we will follow in the paw prints of many great Dogedin mayors that have come before us. My goal as your new mayor is to provide my four-legged friends a safe and happy place to live. Every dish will have a bone, every bowl will have water, and every pet will have a loving home in Dogedin as long as I am mayor. Thanks again for all of your barks and wags!

The End

Scotty is excited to be the Mayor of Dogedin!
He hid A SUPERSTAR on every picture! Can
you find them?

Glossary

Ballot: a sheet of paper used to cast a secret vote

Campaign Manager: to coordinate a political campaigns operations such as fundraising, advertising, and getting out the vote

City Hall: a building where government officials work

Citizen: an inhabitant of a particular town or city

County: a division of a state or country for local government

Deputy Mayor: Serves as Mayor when the Mayor is away on vacation

Dogedin: a coastal city of dogs

Election: an organized choice by vote for a political office

Mayor: an official elected to act as the chief executive of a city or town

Treasurer: a guardian of a collection of treasures

CPSIA information can be obtained
at www.ICGtesting.com
Printed in the USA
LVHW072056151021
700578LV00008B/637